CHINESE IMMIGRANTS
IN THEIR SHOES

BY JANIE HAVEMEYER

Published by The Child's World®
1980 Lookout Drive • Mankato, MN 56003-1705
800-599-READ • www.childsworld.com

Content Consultant: Ping Xu, Associate Professor, Department of Political Science,
University of Rhode Island

ISBN 9781503827967
LCCN 2018944111

Printed in the United States of America
PA02394

ABOUT THE AUTHOR

Janie Havemeyer is an author of many books for young readers. She lives in
San Francisco, California, and has visited Angel Island. Janie loves history
and learning about the lives of other people. For many years she taught
California history to third graders. She is a graduate of Middlebury College
and Bank Street College of Education.

TABLE OF CONTENTS

FAST FACTS

Early Chinese Immigrants

- In 1851, approximately 2,700 Chinese immigrants lived in San Francisco, California. As word about the discovery of gold spread throughout China, more immigrants came. In 1852, more than 20,000 Chinese immigrants had arrived in San Francisco.

- In 1882, the U.S. government began to regulate the entry of Chinese immigrants into the United States.

- In 1910, an immigration station was built on the north shore of Angel Island in San Francisco Bay. All immigrants entering the United States by way of the Pacific Ocean went here.

Chinese Students and Professionals

- New immigration laws in 1990 allowed more skilled and educated Chinese immigrants to come to the United States as temporary workers. Also, beginning in the 1990s, adopted children from China began arriving in the United States.

- In 2014, approximately 274,000 Chinese students arrived to study in the United States.

TIMELINE

1848: Gold is discovered in California. Many Chinese come to the United States to seek their fortune.

1882: The Chinese **Exclusion** Act limits Chinese immigration to the United States for ten years. Chinese immigrants cannot become citizens during this time. The Chinese Exclusion Act is renewed in 1892 for another ten years, and again in 1902 with no end date.

1910–1940: Angel Island Immigration Station operates. Approximately 175,000 Chinese immigrants pass through the station.

1943: The ban on Chinese immigration is finally lifted.

1965: The United States allows up to 20,000 immigrants from all countries around the world to move to the United States each year. This begins another wave of Chinese immigration to the United States.

1980s: A new, open relationship between the United States and China brings another wave of Chinese immigrants to the United States that continues into the 2000s.

Chapter 1

EARLY IMMIGRANTS

Wong Hoy Fung strolled the six blocks of San Francisco's Dai Fou neighborhood. Americans called this neighborhood Chinatown because it was where all the Chinese immigrants lived. Men with long **queues** chatted loudly. People rushed from store to store, buying dried fish or duck or selecting the right herbs for cooking. In China, Fung had dreamed of finding a better life in the United States.

◄ **Many Chinese immigrants hoped for good work opportunities in the United States.**

Chinese people had said that "Money is in great plenty and to spare in America" and that California needed more laborers to build the west.[1] But after Fung arrived in 1876, he discovered there was a lot of competition for work. Also, Californians treated the Chinese badly. They called them "the Yellow Peril."[2] Americans worried these hard-working people would steal all the jobs. A year after Fung arrived, an anti-Chinese riot broke out in Chinatown. A mob set fire to buildings and shot Chinese bystanders in the streets.

"I heard people say that Gold Mountain [California] was a good place. Like going to heaven. But you really don't know until you are there. It's been a hard life."[3]

—*Jew Law Ying, Chinese American immigrant who arrived in San Francisco in 1941*

Fung found a job in the city of Los Angeles, California. The Southern Pacific Railroad needed men to lay tracks from Los Angeles to Texas. It was hard work. Shoulder to shoulder, hour after hour in the sun, Fung worked with other Chinese people.

▲ **While working on the railroad, Chinese workers would camp near the construction zone.**

They cleared a path for the train track. Fung breathed in dust, loosened rocks, cut down trees, and dug up their roots until he was numb with exhaustion. But now he could save up enough money to send to his wife and young son back home.

Once the tracks were built, Fung returned to Dai Fou. Many of his countrymen now worked in factories making items such as shoes and cigars. Other Chinese people owned laundries. Fung found work washing clothes. To make more money, he sold lottery tickets door to door. But no matter how hard he worked, he was always poor.

Soon, life became even harder for Chinese immigrants. In 1882, the U.S. government passed laws that affected Chinese people. They were not allowed to become citizens and they were barred from certain jobs. One popular leader, Denis Kearney, ended all his speeches by saying, "The Chinese must go."[4] Angry mobs forced Chinese residents out of many western cities.

One day, a fortune teller told Fung he would not live beyond the age of 60. Fung didn't want to die in California, so he sailed back to China. Life in the United States had not been so golden after all.

▲ **Many Chinese immigrants opened their own businesses in San Francisco's Chinatown.**

Chapter 2

A MERCHANT'S SON

Thirteen-year-old Lee Show Nam sat in the front of the ferryboat with his mother in 1935. Lee felt seasick as the boat crossed the choppy waters of San Francisco Bay. Soon he spotted a cluster of wooden buildings on an island called Angel Island. There was a barbed wire fence surrounding the buildings. Lee remembered his father's warning about this new place. He told him to beware of the *luk yi*. They were American inspectors.

◄ **Angel Island Immigration Station closed in 1940 and is now a museum.**

They would decide if a person could enter the United States. Lee's father said they would try to trick him with their questions.

Angel Island Immigration Station was the final stop on Lee's month-long voyage from China to California. His father, Lum Piu, was a merchant who lived in California. More than 50 years earlier, the United States had passed the Chinese Exclusion Act. This law barred most Chinese immigrants from coming to the United States but allowed merchants to bring over their families.

On the island, Lee said goodbye to his mother. Because he was older than 12, he had to live by himself in the Chinese men's dormitory until it was his turn to be interrogated by the inspectors. He sat on his white bunk bed, taking deep breathes to calm down. There were poems written on the walls. One said, "Even if it is built of jade, it has turned into a cage."[5]

"When we arrived they locked us up like criminals in compartments like the cages in the zoo."[6]

—*Angel Island immigrant, 1922*

▲ **Carvings of Chinese poetry are still found on some Angel Island walls.**

As time passed, Lee found that each day had the same routine. He would wake up at five o'clock in the morning, then eat breakfast an hour later. Lunch was at ten o'clock, and dinner was at three. There were many rules to follow. Once, Lee forgot one.

▲ **Women and children were kept at Angel Island Immigration Station for long periods of time.**

He didn't shut off the water faucet in the bathroom and was locked in a dark closet by one of the officers in charge of rule breakers. Lee tried not to cry. Instead, he practiced answering the questions he thought the *luk yi* would ask. His father had given him a coaching book to prepare. The *luk yi* might ask, "What are the birth and marriage dates of your family members?" or "How many steps lead up to your house [in China]?"[7] His father said that if Lee gave the wrong answers, Lee could be sent back to China.

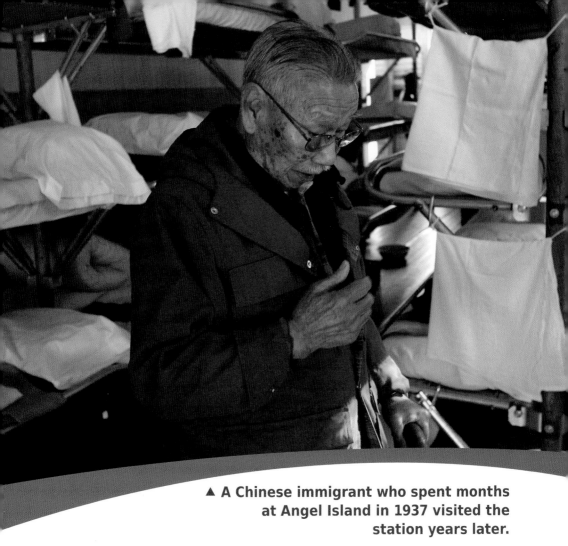

▲ A Chinese immigrant who spent months at Angel Island in 1937 visited the station years later.

On his tenth day in the United States, it was finally Lee's turn to meet the inspectors. He sat in an office with two of them and an **interpreter**. He gripped his hands together to keep them from shaking. Over four days Lee answered hundreds of questions. One inspector eyed him suspiciously. He said he didn't look anything like his father. Finally, the inspectors reached their decision. They accused Lee of lying about being his father's son.

They called him a **paper son**—the name for immigrants who pretended to be the sons of Chinese Americans. Lee didn't understand. He'd told only the truth.

Lee's father fought back against the ruling by hiring a lawyer. Lee and his mother waited, locked up on the island. After 18 months, they lost their case and were sent back to China. Lee tried to move to the United States again in 1963. This time he came by plane. His papers were in order, and no one asked him any questions when he arrived. But he was sad it had taken him 28 years to join his father.

Tyrus Wong and his father were only two of 175,000 Chinese immigrants held and interrogated at the Angel Island Immigration Station between 1910 and 1940. These are some of the personal belongings that Tyrus's father brought with him on his journey from China.

▲ **Some California museums have the belongings of Chinese immigrants who passed through Angel Island.**

Chapter 3

ACCUSATIONS

One spring morning in 1955, Tung Pok Chin was busy ironing shirt collars using his collar presser. Steam rose up as he pressed down on the cotton. A drop of sweat fell from his forehead. Then he heard voices at his door. Two men dressed in suits stepped into the laundry he owned. Winifred, Chin's three-year old daughter, scurried over to hide behind his legs. The men introduced themselves as Federal Bureau of Investigation (FBI) agents.

◀ The U.S. House Un-American Activities Committee questioned people it suspected had ties to Communists.

They asked if his name was Lai Bing Chan. Chin's heart started pounding. Lai Bing Chan was his name when he lived in China, but in the United States he'd pretended to be Tung Pok Chin. He was a paper son. "[I'm] Tung Pok Chin," he replied as calmly as he could.[8]

"Mr. Chin, we have reason to believe that you are a **communist**," the tall FBI agent said.[9] A wave of panic filled Chin's body. He might be able to fool these men about his true identity, but being called a Communist was very serious. A few years earlier, China had become a Communist country. The United States thought Communism was a threat to its democracy and had begun to hunt for Communists. Chinese immigrants were immediately suspected because they had family ties in China.

Chin took a deep breath. "I am not a communist. I belong to no party," he said. But throughout the morning, the agents kept grilling him. They asked him questions such as, "Do you subscribe to the pro-communist paper the *China Daily News*?" and "Do you know Lai Bing Chan?"[10] Chin swallowed. He had been publishing poems in the paper under his name Lai Bing Chan. It was the only place he had ever used his real name. Writing poetry meant the world to him.

"I do not see the harm in anyone writing a few poems," he answered, pretending not to know Lai Bing Chan.[11] He kept doing his chores to appear relaxed. Finally, the agents left. But Chin knew they'd be back.

That night, he threw out all his old copies of the *China Daily News*. He burned his scrapbooks with all his poems. Black smoke rose from the curling papers. He cried as the books went up in flames. They had been a record of his life in the United States. But he couldn't keep them. It was too risky.

"I could not hold back the tears as I watched my life's work literally go up in flames. I once had visions of binding my poetry into a book for publication. Perhaps some Chinese American scholar would come across it and translate it into English, I thought. With such a detailed record of immigrant life, the old home town, the history and emotions of the paper son, I would really gain recognition as a poet! But now, all was lost."[12]

—*Tung Pok Chin on destroying his poems*

◄ **Chinese Communists established the People's Republic of China in 1949. Mao Zedong was a Communist leader.**

If the government thought he was Lai Bing Chan or a Communist, he would be sent back to China.

After the FBI visit, Chin began to notice things. His mail had been opened and resealed. His phone made a funny clicking sound. So he stopped writing letters and poetry. He made his home look "as American as possible" to prove his **patriotism**.[13] He put out only American magazines. Finally, after five years, the FBI visits stopped. The panic over Communist spies in the United States had declined.

Afterward, Chin found the courage to write poetry again. One day, Winifred brought home two poems she had been studying in her university class. Chin recognized his poetry. His work had been discovered in old copies of the *China Daily News*. A smile lit his face when he realized he was now being honored as a poet in the United States.

In 1972, President Richard Nixon (left) visited the People's ▶ Republic of China to build better relationships with its leaders. He met with China's leader Zhou Enlai (right).

Chapter 4

A NEW BEGINNING

On the first day of school, Jubilee Lau held tightly to her father's hand as he walked her inside Centennial Elementary School in Nampa, Idaho. A cool gust from the air conditioning made her shiver. All around her she saw students with faces different from her own. But everyone smiled at her. Jubilee felt a little better. She had spent the last few weeks hiding in her new house in Nampa. At night, Jubilee had nightmares about speaking English.

◀ Educational opportunities open many doors for people.

Everyone spoke it so fast here, and Jubilee never understood what they were saying.

Jubilee and her family had moved to the United States from Hong Kong in 1983 and settled first in San Francisco. Jubilee's parents said the United States was the land of opportunities, where Jubilee could get the best education. Since 1965, new rules allowed more Chinese families like theirs to move to the United States.

In her new classroom, Jubilee's teacher spoke slowly to her. "You are the only Asian we've ever had in this school, and we hope you'll feel right at home." The other students crowded around Jubilee. They asked her, "Are you from China?" and "Say something in Chinese!"[14]

Jubilee took a deep breath. Everyone seemed excited to meet her. She answered the volley of questions. No one cared that her English was not great. By the end of the day, she felt a little better.

It didn't take long for Jubilee to become fluent in English. She won a spelling bee. She also learned to play the jump rope game Double Dutch at recess. Her classmates asked her more questions about China. They begged Jubilee to teach them some Chinese.

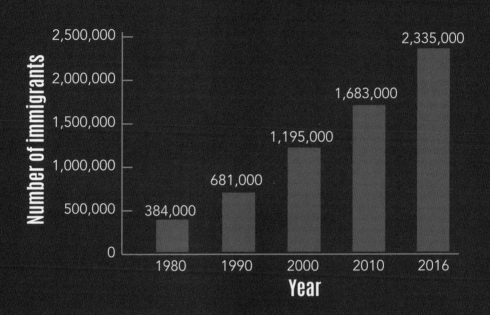

CHINESE IMMIGRANT POPULATION (1980-2016)

Jubilee felt proud of her heritage. She'd said she had "never felt so good" about herself.[15] Her parents were proud of her, too. They knew Jubilee was going to make something of her life in the United States.

◀ **Some immigrants leave their home country because they hope their children will have a better life in the United States.**

Chapter 5

AN AMERICAN EDUCATION

Heiying "Haddy" Zhang tossed the small white ball into the air. With her right hand she swung her paddle and connected with the ball. The ball shot low over the net. Her opponent dove for it, and the ball bounced back. With a quick flip of her wrist, Haddy aimed the ball so it landed in the far-right corner of the ping-pong table. She had scored a point!

◄ **Thousands of Chinese students come to the United States for college.**

Haddy had left the bustling city of Beijing, China, in 2015 to attend the University of Iowa. Table tennis, or ping-pong, was something she played to escape the pressures of university life. As a Chinese student going to school in the United States, there were many new things for her to figure out. She counted on the other Chinese students, and her new American friends, Jarol and Leah Duerksen, to help her.

Haddy's parents wanted her to earn a college degree. Like many middle- and upper-class Chinese families, the Zhangs saw education as the path to success. Many Chinese believed the United States had the best universities. Haddy's parents sold their spare apartment in Beijing to afford her education.

At first, Haddy was surprised when she drove through Iowa. It seemed like there were never-ending rows of green cornfields.

"I have [Chinese] roommates who are afraid to talk to Americans, and I ask them, 'What's the point of coming all the way to America if you're not going to talk to anybody here?'"[16]

—*Fan Yijia, a Chinese student at the University of Iowa*

▲ **China has many famous table tennis players.**

In Beijing, there were tall buildings everywhere. Haddy felt more at home hanging out with the other Chinese students, and some days she spoke only **Mandarin**. She knew she needed to practice speaking English, but it was a struggle to find the right words. Writing papers was worse. She was afraid of making mistakes that would get her into trouble. Sometimes the pressure boiled up. But her parents were counting on her. Haddy believed giving up was not an option.

But every Wednesday night, Haddy visited her American friends, Jarol and his wife, Leah. She played competitive ping-pong at their house with other Chinese students. When she showed up, Jarol shouted, "You made it!" because he was happy to see her.[17] In the house, a world map covered in pins showed the place from which each student had traveled to get to Iowa.

Haddy was one of many Chinese immigrants who looked for new opportunities in the United States. Although it was difficult at times, Haddy continued to do her best to build a life in an unfamiliar country.

THINK ABOUT IT

- How do you think immigrants such as Lee Show Nam and his mother felt being detained on Angel Island?
- What types of difficulties and challenges have Chinese immigrants faced in the United States? Do you think their experience is similar to or different from other immigrants? Explain your answer.
- How do you think immigrants feel when they move to a country and can't speak the country's official language?

GLOSSARY

Communist (KOM-yuh-nist): Communist describes an economic, political, and social system controlled by the state. China established its first Communist state in 1949.

exclusion (ek-SKLOO-zhun): Exclusion is the act of shutting or keeping something or someone out. Chinese immigrants faced exclusion from the U.S. government for many years.

interpreter (in-TUR-prit-er): An interpreter is a person who translates out loud for people speaking different languages. Some Chinese immigrants had help from an interpreter.

Mandarin (MAN-dur-in): Mandarin is the chief language of China. Haddy Zhang spoke Mandarin in the United States.

paper son (PAY-pur SUN): A paper son was a Chinese immigrant who pretended to be the child of someone else to get into a country illegally. Lee Show Nam couldn't get into the United States because officials thought he was a paper son.

patriotism (PAY-tree-uh-tism): Patriotism is a love for one's country. Tung Pok Chin wanted to prove his patriotism to the FBI.

queues (KYOOS): Queues are pigtails usually worn hanging at the back of the head and down the back. Many Chinese immigrants in the 1800s wore their hair in queues.

SOURCE NOTES

1. Erika Lee. *The Making of Asian America: A History*. New York, NY: Simon & Schuster, 2015. Print. 59.

2. Iris Chang. *The Chinese in America*. New York, NY: Viking, 2003. Print. 127.

3. Judy Yung. *Unbound Voices: A Documentary History of Chinese Women in San Francisco*. Berkeley, CA: University of California Press, 1999. Print. 92.

4. "Denis Kennedy." *PBS*. The West Film Project, n.d. Web. 29 June 2018.

5. Ling Woo Liu. "The Other Ellis Island." *Time*. Time, 22 Jan. 2009. Web. 29 June 2018.

6. Ronald T. Takaki. *Strangers from a Different Shore: A History of Asian Americans*. Boston, MA: Little, Brown, 1998. Print. 237.

7. Erika Lee. *Angel Island: Immigrant Gateway to America*. New York, NY: Oxford University Press, 2010. Print. 85.

8. Tung Pok Chin. *Paper Son: One Man's Story*. Philadelphia, PA: Temple University Press, 2000. Print. 68.

9. Ibid. 69.

10. Ibid. 69.

11. Ibid. 70.

12. Ibid. 75.

13. Ibid. 95–96.

14. Judy Yung, Gordon H. Chang, and Him Mark Lai, eds. *Chinese American Voices: from the Gold Rush to the Present*. Berkeley, CA: University of California Press, 2006. Print. 366.

15. Ibid.

16. Brook Larmer. "Alienation 101." *Economist*. Economist Newspaper Limited, April/May 2017. Web. 29 June 2018.

17. Ibid.

TO LEARN MORE

Books

Branscombe, Allison. *All About China*. Tokyo, JP: Tuttle Publishing, 2014.

Wilson, Steve. *The California Gold Rush: Chinese Laborers in America (1848–1882)*. New York, NY: PowerKids Press, 2016.

Yomtov, Nelson. *China*. New York, NY: Children's Press, 2018.

Web Sites

Visit our Web site for links about Chinese immigrants: childsworld.com/links

Note to Parents, Teachers, and Librarians: We routinely verify our Web links to make sure they are safe and active sites. So encourage your readers to check them out!

INDEX